HIU.

Danny's Secret Fox

SUSAN GATES

Illustrated by
Alicia Garcia de Lynam

OXFORD
UNIVERSITY PRESS

OXFORD
UNIVERSITY PRESS

Great Clarendon Street, Oxford OX2 6DP

Oxford University Press is a department of the University of Oxford.
It furthers the University's objective of excellence in research, scholarship,
and education by publishing worldwide in

Oxford   New York
Auckland   Cape Town   Dar es Salaam   Hong Kong   Karachi
Kuala Lumpur   Madrid   Melbourne   Mexico City   Nairobi
New Delhi   Shanghai   Taipei   Toronto

With offices in
Argentina   Austria   Brazil   Chile   Czech Republic   France   Greece
Guatemala   Hungary   Italy   Japan   Poland   Portugal   Singapore
South Korea   Switzerland   Thailand   Turkey   Ukraine   Vietnam

Oxford is a registered trade mark of Oxford University Press
in the UK and in certain other countries

British Library Cataloguing in Publication Data
Data available

ISBN-13: 978-0-19-918408-8
ISBN-10: 0-19-918408-9

5 7 9 10 8 6 4

Available in packs
Stage 14 Pack of 6:
ISBN-13: 978-0-19-918406-4; ISBN-10: 0-19-918406-2
Stage 14 Class Pack:
ISBN-13: 978-0-19-918413-2; ISBN-10: 0-19-918413-5
Guided Reading Cards also available:
ISBN-13: 978-0-19-918415-6; ISBN-10: 0-19-918415-1

Cover artwork by Alicia Garcia de Lynam
Photograph of Susan Gates © Pauline Holbrook

Printed in Great Britain by
Ashford Colour Press, Gosport Hants

CHAPTER 1

The night visitor

'Do you want to know something amazing?' asked Danny's dad.

'No,' said Danny. He was hardly ever in a good mood at breakfast time.

'Last night at work,' said Danny's dad, 'a fox came in through the big main gates. It just walked right in, when they opened them up for a lorry.'

Danny stopped crunching his cornflakes. He put down his spoon. 'What, just walked right in?' he asked.

He couldn't help sounding surprised. Dad worked the night shift at a chemical factory. Danny had been there once, just to look at it. It was an eerie place, right out on the edge of town. It had a high wire fence around it. 'DANGER,' it said on the fence. 'KEEP OUT.'

At night the factory was all lit up. You could see it for miles around. Great long pipes snaked in all directions. Huge vats hissed and bubbled. It smelled like rotten eggs.

'That place gives me the creeps,' shivered Danny. 'That fox must be brave, to go in there.'

'Or starving,' said Dad.

He went on, 'I threw it a cheese sandwich. It gulped it down as if it hadn't eaten for weeks. It looks very young – not much more than a cub really.'

Danny grunted and went back to his cornflakes.

But after that, when Dad came in from work, Danny always asked about the fox.

The fox came every night to the chemical factory. It waited for the big gates to open and strolled in with the lorries. It wasn't scared of their great rumbling wheels.

'Too young and stupid to be scared,' said Danny's dad.

CHAPTER 2

The fox with fiery eyes

One Saturday morning, when Danny was still in bed, his dad came in from work. He poked his head round the bedroom door.

'Guess what? You'll never guess what that cheeky young devil did last night?'

'What cheeky young devil?' yawned Danny.

'The fox!' said Dad. 'Last night it came right up to me. It ate a cheese sandwich right out of my hand.'

Suddenly Danny was wide awake. 'Wow! Really?'

'Yes, it's getting very tame – and choosy. Now it just eats the cheese slice and leaves the bread behind.'

'I didn't know foxes liked cheese slices,' said Danny.

'This one does.'

'Can I come and feed it?' begged Danny. 'Just once? Please?'

'No way,' said Dad. 'They don't let children in the factory. It's too dangerous. You know that.'

But, next night, Dad took a photo of the fox, with his Instamatic camera.

'Look at its eyes!' cried Danny, amazed. The fox's eyes were glowing with green fire!

'Oh, that's just the flash on the camera,' explained his dad. 'It doesn't really look like that.'

But Danny wasn't listening. He put the photo in his pocket.

He wanted more than ever to feed the fox – the magic fox with fiery eyes. The hero fox, who wasn't scared by the factory with its hissing pipes and stinking, bubbling vats.

But then it seemed as though his chance had gone. They closed down the chemical factory. Danny's dad was lucky. He got a new job in another factory. But in all the upset and confusion everyone forgot about the fox. Except Danny.

And one day, he set out on his bike to see if it was still there. It was winter now, dark nights, and he was only allowed out until five o'clock. He took cheese sandwiches, wrapped up in silver foil, just as his dad had done.

And he told nobody where he was going. The fox was his secret now.

Danny leaned his bike up against an empty oil drum.

It was a wasteland where the factory had been. The buildings were like empty shells. All the windows had been smashed. Soon bulldozers would move in and flatten the whole lot.

Danny crouched down behind a pile of bricks.

'That fox won't come,' he was thinking. 'I might as well go home.'

But just as he was wheeling his bike away, he saw the young fox. It was picking its way through the rubble.

It wasn't as red and sleek as Danny had imagined. In fact, you could easily mistake it for a mangy dog. And when it moved closer, he saw that its eyes were brown, not green and fiery.

But, somehow, that didn't matter.

Danny tugged his sandwich from his pocket. Very gently, he leaned his bike against the oil drum so it didn't clang and scare the fox away. Then he crouched down, hardly daring to breathe.

The fox came closer. 'Brave fox,' said Danny softly. 'Come on, brave fox.'

It was so close now that Danny caught a whiff of its strong, foxy scent.

There!

The fox had whipped the sandwich right out of Danny's fingers. And just as Dad had said, it dropped the sandwich on the ground. It twitched the cheese slice out with its sharp, pointed teeth.

'Wow!' whispered Danny, thrilled.

The fox turned and stared at him. Then it was off, trotting like a little dog through the wasteland.

'I'll come and feed you every day. I'll look after you. I won't tell anybody,' Danny promised the fox. 'You'll be my secret.'

The secret fox slid away into the grey evening light. One whisk of a furry tail and it was gone.

But the very next day Danny broke his promise.

CHAPTER 3

Danny breaks his promise

It was because of Scott. Scott was big and clumsy. People at school were scared of him – he had no friends. Scott had spiky hair and a scowling face. And he was always trying to pick fights. Sensible people kept right out of his way.

He was trying to pick a fight with Danny now. 'You're too scared to fight,' Scott sneered at Danny. 'You're too scared to do anything! You wimp!'

'No, I'm not!' said Danny. He knew he should have walked away, like a sensible person. He knew he should have kept his mouth shut. But he couldn't help himself.

'I feed a fox. I can feed it right out of my hand. Like this!' And Danny stretched out his arm to show how he fed the fox. 'I've tamed it. All on my own. You couldn't do that! Could you? Could you?'

And Danny even dragged the photo out of his pocket and shoved it under Scott's nose.

'Look there, if you don't believe me!'

Scott scowled. He peered at the photo: 'Where is this fox then?'

'Down at the old factory,' boasted Danny. 'Where my dad used to work.'

He could have kicked himself. 'You fool!' he told himself.

And then he thought, 'Perhaps Scott doesn't know where it is.'

But Scott did know. 'I know where that is,' he said. 'My big brother's got an air rifle. He likes shooting things. I'll tell him about your fox!'

That night Danny cycled down to the wasteland. But he didn't have any cheese sandwiches with him. Instead, he leaned his bike against the oil drum.

He picked up some big stones. Then he piled them beside him and sat, waiting.

He couldn't see anyone else about. There was nobody with an air rifle. But one night, Danny was sure, Scott's big brother would come down here looking for some target practice.

'You and your big mouth!' Danny said angrily to himself as he crouched there, shivering.

He knew what he had to do.

There it was, the young fox. It was trotting confidently round a pile of bricks, looking for Danny. It was expecting cheese sandwiches.

But Danny stood up. 'Clear off!' he screamed. 'Clear off and don't come back here any more.'

Then Danny threw the first stone. The fox yelped in pain and surprise. It backed off. Danny chucked another and another.

'Go away. It's not safe here any more!'

Danny chased his fox, howling at it, shrieking. The young fox went streaking through the rubble. Danny stumbled after, pelting everything he could lay his hands on. But most of the stones missed. You can't aim very well when your eyes are full of tears.

The next day at school Scott said, 'I was lying about the air rifle. You didn't believe me, did you? Everybody knows I haven't got a big brother. I've only got a baby sister. Ha, ha, ha!'

Danny cycled to the factory the next night and the next. But the fox didn't come back. Danny felt empty inside. And very sad, as if he'd lost something precious. All he had left was the photo of the fox. He kept it in his pocket. And, now and again, he took it out to look at those magical, fiery eyes.

But then even that was gone. He left the photo in the pocket of his jeans and Mum washed them. The photo became a handful of grey, soggy pieces.

CHAPTER 4

Scott

Winter turned into spring. Spring turned into early summer. The nights were lighter now and Danny was allowed out until seven o'clock. But he hadn't cycled down to the factory for weeks. Now his fox had gone, there was nothing to go there for.

'Serves you right!' Danny told himself. 'You told Scott about the secret fox. You spoiled everything!'

Then, one evening, Danny set out on his bike for the wasteland. He was looking for some wood to build a go-kart. Go-karts were the latest craze. All the kids were making them.

He cycled round a corner. And he nearly rode slap bang into Scott who was crouching in the road.

'Oh no,' thought Danny, braking like mad. 'I'm for it now!'

He skidded to a halt. His front wheel brushed Scott's brand-new white trainers. It left a muddy mark.

'Escape! Escape!' Danny's brain screamed at him. 'Ride like the wind! Maybe he won't know it's you!'

But it was too late to escape. Scott was already talking to him.

'You silly, silly little sparrow,' said Scott.

'What's that?' said Danny warily, staring down at Scott's spiky head. 'What did you say just then?'

Scott scowled up at him. He seemed puzzled to see Danny there. He didn't seem to know he'd almost been run over.

'I'm talking to this sparrow,' he told Danny.

Danny gulped. You never knew where you were with Scott. You couldn't tell what he was thinking. He might decide to get mad with you. Or he might not.

Danny waited.

'Look,' said Scott, 'at this silly little sparrow. It's gone and broke its wing.'

Scott's hands were big and clumsy like a bear's paws. He held them up to Danny. Cupped in Scott's hands was a baby sparrow. One of its wings was useless. It was broken, spread out like a fan.

'What are you going to do with it?' asked Danny. 'You're not going to hurt it, are you?'

He'd said the wrong thing. He jumped back as Scott roared, ''Course I'm not going to hurt it! I'm going to take it home with me, aren't I? I'm going to set its wing, make it better. Then I'll let it go again.'

Danny was so surprised that he forgot to be scared of Scott. He was surprised too, how gentle Scott was with the sparrow. He had never seen Scott gentle before. Only scary.

'Can you really do that?' asked Danny. 'Can you mend its wing?'

'My dad showed me,' said Scott. 'You use a lolly stick as a splint. And you feed them water out of an eye-dropper. And you give 'em tiny worms with tweezers.'

Scott stroked the sparrow's head very, very gently with his fingernail. It cheeped at him. It opened its pale yellow beak very wide.

'You'll be all right,' Scott told the sparrow. 'Don't be scared. I'll look after you.'

He got up out of the road. The baby sparrow was cradled tenderly in his great, bear's paw hands.

Danny felt his mouth hanging open. He couldn't help it.

Then, as if he knew what Danny was thinking, Scott said, 'I like animals, see? Animals are all right.'

'Wait a minute,' said Danny. 'If you like animals, why did you say all that about your brother shooting my fox?'

'I told you,' said Scott. 'I haven't got a brother. I like foxes. I wouldn't let anyone shoot them.'

'But why did you *say* it?' asked
Danny again. He knew it was risky,
challenging Scott like this. But he
couldn't help it. He couldn't help
thinking about how he'd driven away
his fox. All because of what Scott had
said.

'I don't know,' said Scott miserably.
'I don't know why I said it. I just get
like that sometimes.' And he gave a sad,
puzzled shake of his head, as if it was a
big mystery to him.

Danny watched Scott shamble off,
carrying the sparrow with the broken
wing. Danny's mouth was still hanging
open. He could hardly believe what
he'd just seen.

'If I told them at school,' thought
Danny, 'about Scott and that baby
sparrow, they'd think I'd gone crazy!'

But he had no time to think about that now. It was getting late. He had to get to the wasteland and find that wood for his go-kart. And get back home before seven o'clock.

He jumped back on his bike.

He had to cycle through a ring of bulldozers. Like great yellow monsters they crouched round the edge of the wasteland. They were waiting for tomorrow. Tomorrow, they would move in and flatten what was left of the buildings.

Danny propped his bike against the empty oil drum.

'There's a good bit!' he thought, pouncing on a piece of wood.

Then, out of the corner of his eye, he saw a movement, behind a pile of bricks.

He looked again. It was only a skinny stray dog, a brown one.

No, it wasn't.

'You came back!'

It was Danny's fox, looking for food.

CHAPTER 5

Fox in danger

The fox came closer. It sniffed at Danny's hand.

'It knows who I am,' thought Danny, thrilled to bits. 'It remembers me!'

'I didn't mean it,' Danny told the fox, 'when I threw stones at you. It's too hard to explain. But I didn't mean it, honest.'

The fox licked his hand, as if it understood.

In his excitement, Danny dropped the piece of wood. He wasn't interested in go-karts any more.

'Wait, wait there!' he told his fox. 'Don't go away.' He grabbed his bike. 'I'll be back. I promise.'

'Cheese sandwiches,' he was thinking, as he pedalled home. 'I hope there's lots of cheese slices in our fridge!'

He flung his bike down by the back door, skidded into the kitchen, yanked open the fridge.

'Great!' He pulled out a handful of cheese slices and dashed towards the back door.

He was halfway through it when a voice said: 'And just where do you think you're going?'

It was Mum, looking cross, tapping her watch: 'Do you know what time it is?' she said. 'You're ten minutes late. It's ten past seven!'

'Oh please, Mum, please. The fox is back. I've got to go. Got to go right now and feed him.' Danny was leaping about with impatience. 'Please Mum, can I come in at eight tonight? Please, Mum, just this once. I've got really important things to do!'

But Mum would not budge. 'No way,' she said. 'Rules are rules. If I let you stay out until eight tonight, it'll be eight-thirty tomorrow night and nine the night after –'

'It won't, it won't, I promise!'

It was no good. Danny tried every trick he knew. He nagged and begged and pleaded. He told his mum she was the best mum in the world. But it was still no good. So he stomped off to bed. And all night long he fretted. He tossed and turned. He couldn't sleep. He was desperate to go and feed his fox.

'He'll think I'm not coming!' Danny thought, over and over again.

Next morning, as soon as Mum would let him, Danny zoomed out of the house. He stuffed some cheese slices in his coat pocket. He pedalled so fast his wheels were just a blur.

He was almost at the wasteland when he saw Scott. Scott was all on his own, as usual. He was always on his own.

Danny didn't stop.

It flashed through his mind that he'd like to ask Scott about the baby sparrow. But he didn't stop. For one thing, he didn't have time. And, for another thing, he still wasn't sure about Scott. What if Scott said, 'You talking to me?' and acted as if he'd never cradled a sick baby bird in his hands?

What then?

So Danny pedalled on.

He heard the noise before he saw the wasteland. It was an angry, snarling noise, like a whole skyful of wasps.

He turned the corner. The bulldozers had already started work. The yellow monsters had come alive. They were jerking their yellow arms about. They had the old factory surrounded. They were moving in on it. Ready to crunch it in their jaws.

And somewhere, lost in all that noise and dust, was Danny's fox.

Danny threw his bike to the ground. He looked round frantically. But all he could see were roaring machines. No fox. Where was his fox?

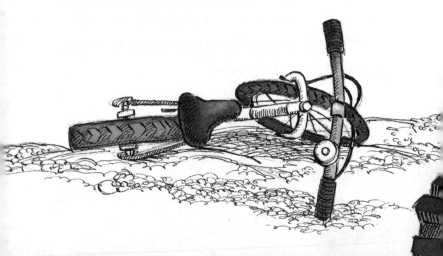

And then he saw it. His fox was outside the ring of bulldozers. Running to and fro, to and fro. It was frantic, like Danny.

'Get out the way!' Danny called to his fox. If it didn't watch out, the fox would be dragged under those massive wheels. Why didn't it run away? Why was it risking its life?

'Get out the way!' Danny shrieked to his fox, as it tried to dodge past a bulldozer. 'What are you doing? You'll get killed!'

CHAPTER 6

Run!

But the fox made another dash. Great wheels almost crushed it into the dirt. But it leaped out the way. Still it wouldn't run away.

'Run!' yelled Danny, helplessly. But he couldn't even hear his own voice above the roaring machines.

'She's trying to get to her cub,' said a voice in Danny's ear.

Danny jumped round, startled. It was Scott. Scott, the last person in the world Danny wanted to see.

'That fox is a vixen,' said Scott, shouting above the din. 'She's a little vixen. And look, look there. That's her den. Can you see it?'

Danny strained his eyes through the clouds of dust.

'Yes, I can see it!'

There was a hole, like a big rabbit burrow, under an old brick wall. And the bulldozers were heading straight for that wall. They would topple it as if it were made of Lego. And the den would be buried under heaps of bricks.

'I bet she's got a cub in there!' yelled Scott. 'She's trying to save it. But the 'dozers'll get there first.'

'Oh no,' yelled Danny. Out of the
hole came a cub, no bigger than a
kitten. Its legs were wobbly. It stood at
the edge of the den. It began mewing
for its mother.

'Why can't they see it?' cried Danny.
'Why can't the drivers see it?'

But the drivers, high up in their cabs,
didn't see the fox cub. The bulldozers
rolled on.

The vixen, trapped outside the machines, began a high, yelping bark.

The cub heard it and began to totter towards her. Right into the path of the bulldozers.

'I'm going to get it!' shouted Danny. He dashed forward but someone grabbed his coat.

It was Scott. 'Let me go, let me go, you big bully!' cried Danny, struggling to get free.

But Scott was too strong. He pushed Danny over. 'You wait here,' he said. 'I can run faster than you. I'll get it.'

Danny scrambled to his feet.

The machines jerked and crashed forwards. Clouds of dust rose. The vixen's shrill bark went on and on. The cub stopped, bewildered and scared. It started to back away. Too late. Scott was running as if his heart would burst. Too late!

'Come back, Scott!' yelled Danny. 'You can't make it. Come back!'
Danny started to run too.

Then an amazing thing happened.
One bulldozer stopped, its yellow arms
high in the air. Then another cut its
engine. Then another.

The dust died down.

Men in hard hats got out of the
bulldozers and strolled away towards a
little hut. It was tea break time.

There was silence. It was peaceful and
quiet. You could even hear a bird
singing.

Scott walked right into the centre of the ring of bulldozers. There was no danger now – they were as still as statues. He walked up to the little, shivering cub. He bent down. But before he could pick it up the vixen nipped in. She picked the cub up by the scruff of its neck and went trotting off with it.

Danny watched her as she crossed the wasteland. And vanished out of sight.

Scott came back, panting.

'Wow, that was close,' he said.

'That was a crazy thing to do,' said Danny. 'A really dangerous thing to do.'

'You would have done it,' said Scott, 'if I hadn't pushed you over and stopped you. Wouldn't you?'

Danny said nothing. He gave Scott a grin. It was only a quick grin. But it was, sort of, friendly. If you had told Danny that one day, he would grin at Scott in a sort of friendly way, he would have said, 'You're joking!'

Scott said, slowly, 'You're all right, you are.'

That was all he said. But Danny felt pleased, as if Scott had said something really nice about him.

Danny looked out over the wasteland. 'Do you think she'll come back?' he asked Scott.

'I wouldn't,' said Scott, 'if I was her. I'd take that cub somewhere else. Somewhere safe. It's too dangerous here now.'

Danny sighed and closed his eyes. He wished he still had his photo. Then suddenly, he saw a picture in his mind. It was better than any photo. It was a fox. A wonderful fox. A brave, magical fox with green fiery eyes.

And this time it really was Danny's secret fox. It was tucked away in his mind. Where no-one else knew about it.

Scott stood there, waiting quietly, while Danny seemed lost in a dream.

'Do you want to see the sparrow?' asked Scott, suddenly. 'Do you want to see how I fixed its wing?'

Danny opened his eyes.

'I know it's not as good as your fox,' said Scott. 'But it's really tame, see. 'Course, it can't fly yet. But it takes food right out your hand. You could come round to my house and feed it.'

Danny thought about it. He wasn't 100 per cent sure that this was a good idea. Scott looked as big and awkward and scary as he always did. He was shuffling his feet about. His hair stuck out in wild spikes.

But Danny had seen him racing like a champion sprinter to rescue the fox cub. He had seen him shelter a hurt baby bird in those big fists.

'OK,' he said, taking a chance.

Danny picked up his bike. He pushed it with one hand and stuck the other hand in his pocket.

There was something in there. Something horribly soft and squishy.

'This sparrow doesn't eat cheese slices, does it?' Danny asked Scott as they walked away together.

About the author

I was born in Grimsby but I live now in County Durham.

I was an English teacher for ten years before I became a children's writer.

The idea for this book came from a true story.

My brother-in-law, Tony, works in a chemical factory and he told me about a young fox, who came in every night to be fed. Tony even took a photograph of the fox with a flash, so it looked as if it had green fiery eyes. I kept that photo on my desk while I was writing this story.